P9-DEG-147

Just Kidding

by **Trudy Ludwig**   Illustrations by **Adam Gustavson**

Tricycle Press
Berkeley / Toronto

⮞ Foreword ⮜

We have learned through decades of research that there are three ways in which bullying is like other forms of harassment:

It is the result of an imbalance of power. The student who bullies may be bigger, more popular, or may have the implicit support of peers who encourage the harassing behavior.
The bully chooses the bullying behavior. The target does nothing to cause the bullying.
The bully blames the target for the harassment. I.e., "I only call him names because he's such a geek."

Stopping bullying, like stopping sexual harassment, spousal abuse, and racism, takes more than just giving targets advice like, "Don't let it bother you," or "Tell him how you feel when he does that," or "Wear different clothes so they don't stare at you." Giving targets of harassment this kind of advice borders on blaming them for the abuse.

In preventing bullying, renowned bullying expert and researcher Dr. Dan Olweus points us to interventions that change the culture of a school, rather than attempt to change the behavior of the targets. Changing patterns of harassment takes a comprehensive approach, including setting clear standards for acceptable and unacceptable behavior, implementing consistent consequences for actions that are likely to hurt others, and providing education about bullying to every student.

Just Kidding and Trudy Ludwig's other book, *My Secret Bully*, are the best examples I know of what we need to tell young people who are bullied, including:

1. *"It's not your fault."* Targets of bullying need to know that the bully is fully responsible for the harassment, and that nothing the target did or said caused the harassment. Even if the target is different in some way, is overly sensitive to teasing, or has Asperger's syndrome or another disability, the bully still made a choice to tease, threaten, or hit. The bully is the one who did something wrong.

2. *"Here are some things you can try in response to bullying—AND they may not work because the bully may choose not to listen to you."* If we just give young people advice and assume that the advice will work, we leave them stranded if the advice doesn't work. Often adults tell children to say to a bully: *"I felt hurt when you called* *me names.*" What is that young person to do in the very likely event that the bully says, "*Good. That's what I had in mind.*"

3. "*Bullying does hurt.*" After talking with more than 40,000 children around the United States about bullying, I have yet to present at a school where all the students couldn't complete the sentence "*Sticks and stones may break my bones, but words will never hurt me.*" We all know this sentence is untrue. How does it help young people to pretend they are not in pain? Acknowledging the pain of bullying helps targets heal.

4. "*Ask for help from adults when you are bullied—and if you talk to an adult who does not help, keep telling adults until someone does help you.*" First, we must make sure that adults will listen and help. Young people need to know that we welcome their reports of bullying, and that we will take action to protect them from further harassment. Teens tell me that adults have taught them that, as they get older, they are supposed to solve their own problems. To some extent this is true. Yet if someone robs my house, I am not supposed to chase the robber with a gun or try to tell him how I feel. I am supposed to call the police. And if my neighbor's house is being robbed, I am supposed to call the police as well. The police dispatcher would not rebuke me for tattling, saying: "*Are you just trying to get someone in trouble?*" or "*Why don't you mind your own business?*" Adults have created the concept of "tattling," and I believe that it is now our responsibility to get rid of it. A high school student in Ohio made the importance of this responsibility clear to me in a chilling way when he said: "*Being bullied feels bad. That's what revenge is for.*" In recent years we have seen the tragic consequences of young people feeling both angry and helpless. We need to help them see that adults will step up to the plate and stop bullying if their own actions don't work.

Trudy Ludwig's remarkable book, *Just Kidding*, presents these four messages in an accessible way. Young people responded to *My Secret Bully* with enthusiasm, and recognized that the characters are people like them. I am certain that *Just Kidding* will engage children in the same way, helping the targets of bullying and the adults who care about them.

Stan Davis, bullying prevention consultant, founder of www.stopbullyingnow.com, and author of *Schools Where Everyone Belongs: Practical Strategies for Reducing Bullying*.

There are times I hate being a kid. Here I am, waiting to see which team will choose me for some pickup basketball. And the decision rests on a stupid game of Rock Paper Scissors.

"We'll play two out of three," says Vince to Cody. "Loser gets D.J. . . . ready? *Rock . . . paper . . . scissors!*"

T-T
Olive Button
and kids
teasing

That's what I feel like—a "loser." Like I've got a big *L* stamped on my forehead.

"Rock . . . paper . . . scissors!"

Back at my old school, my friends would joke around with me, but they never made me feel like *I* was a joke.

"Rock . . . paper . . . scissors!"

"Hah! You lose, Cody!" says Vince. "D.J.'s on your team."

I look at the guys. Nobody says anything about Vince's dumb way of choosing whose team I'm on. Suddenly, I don't feel like playing and start heading home.

"Hey D.J., where 'ya going?" calls Vince as I walk off the basketball court.

"Home!" I shout.

"What's the matter, D.J. . . . can't you take a joke? I was just kidding."

"Some joke!" I snap back and break into a run.

T-T
Mr.
Thank Faulker
Finding a
space to feel
better

I race across the baseball field, past a bunch of houses that line my street, and to my tree house in our backyard.

"Jerks!" I yell from the tree house. "They're all jerks!"

Then I sit there, thinking back on all the times Vince made fun of me in front of the other kids.

When I first came to Roosevelt Elementary a month ago, Vince seemed friendly enough. But when I tried out for the soccer team he was on, things started to get a little weird between him and me.

"Hey, Vince!" I told him. "Coach Dibbs said I'd be a great goalie for the team!"

T-S
kids can
be mean
teasing

"Did ya hear that guys?" Vince called out. "D.J.'s gonna be our new *girlie*!" And the kids laughed as Vince pranced around the soccer field with a goofy look on his face.

I laughed along with them because Vince was so funny. But it really bugged me that he made a joke instead of congratulating me.

Yesterday morning, when I got on the school bus, I headed to my usual seat—way in the back, next to Vince, Brian, and the other guys. Right when I sat down, Vince asked, "Are you wearing a pajama top to school?"

Before I could answer, he started poking me with his finger, chanting, "D.J.'s wearing pj's! D.J.'s wearing pj's!"

"That's not funny, Vince," I said.

Poke.

"Quit it!"

Poke.

"Knock if off, Vince!"

Poke.

"CUT IT OUT!"

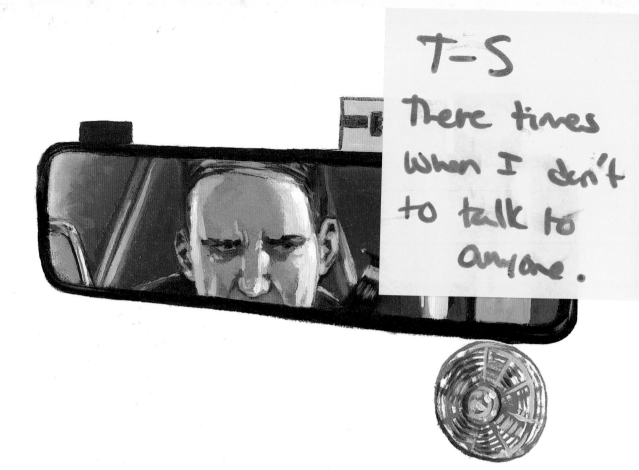

Everyone on the bus got really quiet and the bus driver glared at
Vince and me through his rearview mirror. Vince looked all innocent-like
and said loud enough for the driver to hear, "Geez, I was just kidding!"

Then today Vince comes up with his lame way of placing me on a
team. I've had it!

"D.J., are you in the tree house?" asks Dad from below.

I'm too angry to answer, so I don't.

"D.J. . . . are you okay?"

"I don't want to talk about it!"

"Well, why don't we just play some catch instead?"

I join Dad in the yard and he hands me my baseball glove. We toss the ball in silence. The rhythm of the ball going back and forth calms me down a bit. After a while Dad asks, "You ready to talk about it now?"

"Yeah."

So I tell him how Vince teases me in ways I don't think are funny. "I try to ignore him so he'll stop, but he doesn't," I say. "Then I end up losing it, looking like I'm the jerk because I can't take a joke. I just don't get it, Dad. Why does he pick on me like this?"

"D.J., you may never know exactly why kids like Vince are mean to you. But I do think it has more to do with what's going on with him than with you," he says.

We toss the ball a little more. Then Dad suggests we play a game to help me figure out how to handle myself when kids like Vince pick on me. He calls over my big brother Nick to help. "This game worked for Nick, and I think it'll work for you, too," adds Dad.

"Nick? No way!"

"Yep," nods Nick. "The same kind of thing happened to me at school last year."

"There's only one rule in this game," says Dad. "You can't say or do anything mean back to the teaser."

Nick goes first to show me how the game is played and calls Dad "four eyes."

"You're right," says Dad. "Wearing glasses is like having an extra set of eyes. Thanks for noticing!"

"Good one, Dad!" laughs Nick.

When it's my turn, I can't think of anything great to say, so I just act goofy and that cracks us all up.

The next morning, I get on the school bus and sit down next to Brian. Vince moves to a seat right behind us. I know he's up to no good. Sure enough, he starts making his move—this time on Brian. "Hey, Bed Head!" Vince says. "Did you bother looking in the mirror this morning?" Brian squirms in his seat as some kids on the bus watch in silence.

"Cool 'do," I say to Brian. Then I mess up my hair even worse than Brian's and make a fish face to go with my new, crazy hairdo. The kids around us burst out laughing. Vince doesn't say another word the rest of the ride to school.

"Thanks, D.J.," whispers Brian.

"No problem!" I whisper back.

I'd like to say that Vince stopped bugging me after that, but he didn't. I even caught him red-handed in class, sticking a wad of gum on my chair. When I told him to take it off, he just laughed and walked away.

So my Dad and I met with my teacher, Mrs. Winter, and asked for her advice. Mrs. Winter said she was glad we told her about this problem.

"Vince has somehow learned that it's okay to say and do hurtful things to people," she said. "I'll have the school counselor work with Vince to teach him the skills he needs to be a better friend."

"In the meantime," she adds, "hang out with kids who make you feel good about yourself. It's also important to let me know if Vince continues to pick on you."

"But I don't want to be a tattletale."

"Tattling is when you're trying to get someone in trouble," explained Mrs. Winter. "Reporting is when you're trying to help someone in trouble. In this case, D.J., you're reporting because you're in trouble and you need help."

So I followed Mrs. Winter's advice, and Vince eventually stopped bugging me so much.

Don't get me wrong. It's fun to kid around with your friends and family. But I learned the hard way that when a joke has a sharp edge to it, it can cut you to pieces.

Now I hang out with Brian, Joe, and Miguel. We horse around and have fun—without *making* fun of each other. And that's just the way we like it.

A Note About Teasing

For many families and friends, teasing and kidding around is a way of showing affection and creating a feeling of playful camaraderie with one another. Both the teaser and the person being teased can easily swap roles, there is no imbalance of power, and the basic dignity of everyone involved is maintained. Equally important, if the teaser sees that the person being teased is obviously upset or objects to the teasing, the harmless teaser stops immediately.

When Teasing Is No Laughing Matter

As D.J. in this story found out, "... when a joke has a sharp edge to it, it can cut you to pieces." According to antibullying experts, if a teaser's intent is to hurt, humiliate, ridicule, or demean another person, the teaser has crossed the line into taunting, a form of psychological bullying that can have devastating, long-term negative effects on a child's sense of self.

Obviously, there can be a lot of gray area in this behavioral continuum of teasing vs. taunting; what may be funny to some may be hurtful to others. That's why it's important for adults to be effective role models, and for teachers to help children understand that no joke or teasing remark is ever funny when it's intentionally made at someone else's expense. You're never "just kidding" when your words or actions toward others are embarrassing, hurtful, or mean spirited. A putdown is still a putdown, no matter how you say it.

Discussing The Story

What were some of the mean ways Vince would "kid around" with D.J.?

How could you tell that D.J. was bothered by Vince's teasing?

Why do you think Vince called D.J. a "girlie" instead of congratulating him when D.J. got the goalie position on the soccer team?

When D.J. asked Vince to stop poking him, Vince didn't. How would you feel if someone wouldn't stop doing something that bugged you?

Why do you think Vince continued to tease D.J. when it was obvious D.J. didn't like it?

When Vince said "just kidding," did you believe him? Why or why not?

Do you and your friends tease each other?

How can you tell if your friends like it when you tease them?

How do you let your friends know when their teasing is hurtful?

When do you think teasing is okay and when is it not?

Who can you go to if you have a problem with teasing?

What would you do if you saw other kids teasing your friend in an unkind way?

Additional Resources

ORGANIZATIONS

Girls Incorporated
120 Wall Street, New York, NY 10005-3902 • www.girlsinc.org

Hands & Words Are Not For Hurting Project
P.O. Box 2644, Salem, OR 97308-2644 • www.handsproject.org

Operation Respect
2 Penn Plaza, 5th Floor, New York, NY 10121 • www.operationrespect.org

The Ophelia Project
718 Nevada Drive, Erie, PA 16505 • www.opheliaproject.org

WEBSITES

www.bullying.org
www.cyberbully.org
www.no-bully.com
www.stopbullyingnow.com
www.ifcc.on.ca/bully.htm
www.stopbullyingnow.hrsa.gov/index.asp
www.stopcyberbullying.org

Recommended Readings

FOR ADULTS:
Coloroso, Barbara. *The Bully, the Bullied, and the Bystander*. New York: HarperResource, 2003.
Cooper, Scott. *Sticks and Stones: 7 Ways Your Child Can Deal with Teasing, Conflict, and Other Hard Times*. New York: Random House, 2000.
Davis, Stan. *Schools Where Everyone Belongs: Practical Strategies For Reducing Bullying*. Illinois: Research Press, 2005.
Dellasega, Cheryl, Ph.D., and Charisse Nixon, Ph.D. *Girl Wars: 12 Strategies That Will End Female Bullying*. New York: Simon and Schuster, 2003.
Freedman, Judy. S. *Easing the Teasing: Helping Your Child Cope with Name-Calling, Ridicule, and Verbal Bullying*. New York: McGraw-Hill/Contemporary Books, 2002.
Garbarino, James. *And Words Can Hurt Forever: How to Protect Adolescents from Bullying, Harassment and Emotional Violence*. New York: Free Press, 2003.
Katch, Jane. *They Don't Like Me: Lessons on Bullying and Teasing from a Preschool Classroom*. Massachusetts: Beacon Press, 2003.
McCoy, Elin. *What To Do...When Kids Are Mean To Your Child*. New York: Reader's Digest Adult, 1997.
Thompson, Michael, Lawrence J. Cohen, and Catherine O'Neill Grace. *Best Friends, Worst Enemies: Understanding the Social Lives of Children*. New York: Ballantine Books, 2001.
Thompson, Michael, Lawrence J. Cohen, and Catherine O'Neill Grace. *Mom, They're Teasing Me: Helping Your Child Solve Social Problems*. New York: Ballantine Books, 2002.

FOR CHILDREN:
Burnett, Karen Gedig. *Simon's Hook: A Story About Teases and Putdowns*. California: GR Publishing, 2002.
Cosby, Bill. *The Meanest Thing To Say*. New York: Scholastic Inc., 1997.
Hoose, Phillip and Hannah Hoose. *Hey Little Ant*. California: Tricycle Press, 1998.
Kaufman, Gershen, Raphael, Lev, and Espeland, Pamela. *Stick Up For Yourself! Every Kid's Guide to Personal Power and Positive Self-Esteem*. Minnesota: Free Spirit Publishing, 1999.
Lovell, Patty. *Stand Tall, Molly Lou Melon*. New York: Scholastic Inc., 2002.
Ludwig, Trudy. *My Secret Bully*. California: Tricycle Press, 2005.
Ludwig, Trudy. *Sorry!* California: Tricycle Press, 2006.
Munson, Derek. *Enemy Pie*. California: Chronicle Books, 2000.
Romain, Trevor. *Bullies Are a Pain in the Brain*. Minnesota: Free Spirit Publishing, 1997.
Romain, Trevor. *Cliques, Phonies & other Baloney*. Minnesota: Free Spirit Publishing, 1998.
Seskin, Steve and Allen Shamblin. *Don't Laugh At Me*. California: Tricycle Press, 2002.

For Bennett, Allie, Brad, and mom—with love and respect.
—T.J.L.

For Sean, Scott, Rich, and John.
—A.G.

This is a work of fiction. All names, characters, places, and incidents are either products of the author's imagination or used fictitiously. No reference to any real person is intended or should be inferred. Likeliness of any situations to any persons living or dead is purely coincidental.

Text copyright © 2006 by Trudy Ludwig
Illustrations copyright © 2006 by Adam Gustavson

All rights reserved. No part of this book may be reproduced in any form without the written permission of the publisher, except in the case of brief quotations embodied in critical articles or reviews.

Tricycle Press
an imprint of Ten Speed Press
P.O. Box 7123
Berkeley, California 94707
www.tricyclepress.com

Design by Randall Heath
Typeset in Caslon and Cafeteria
The illustrations in this book were rendered in acrylic paint.

Library of Congress Cataloging-in-Publication Data

Ludwig, Trudy.
Just Kidding / by Trudy Ludwig ; illustrations by Adam Gustavson.
p. cm.
Summary: With help from his father, older brother, and teacher, D.J. learns how to handle a classmate who claims that his mean-spirited "teasing" is just a joke.
ISBN-13: 978-1-58246-163-2 (hardcover)
ISBN-10: 1-58246-163-5 (hardcover)
[1. Bullies--Fiction. 2. Teasing--Fiction. 3. Self-confidence--Fiction.
4. Interpersonal relations--Fiction. 5. Schools--Fiction.] I. Gustavson, Adam, ill. II. Title.
PZ7.L98865Jus 2005   [Fic]--dc22   2005012534
ISBN 1-58246-163-5
First Tricycle Press printing, 2006
Printed in China

3 4 5 6 7 — 11 10 09 08 07

Teasing Dos and Don'ts

DO:

✱ Be careful of others' feelings.

✱ Use humor gently and carefully.

✱ Ask whether teasing about a certain topic hurts someone's feelings.

✱ Accept teasing from others if you tease.

✱ Tell others if teasing about a certain topic hurts your feelings.

✱ Know the difference between friendly, gentle teasing and hurtful ridicule or harassment.

✱ Try to read others' "body language" to see if their feelings are hurt— even when they don't tell you.

✱ Help others when they are being teased or ridiculed.

DON'T:

✱ Tease someone you don't know well.

✱ Tease about a person's body.

✱ Tease about a person's family members.

✱ Tease about a topic when someone asked you not to.

✱ Tease someone who seems agitated or who you know is having a bad day.

✱ Be thin-skinned about teasing that is meant in a friendly way.

✱ Swallow your feelings about teasing. Tell someone in a direct and clear way what is bothering you.

Used with permission from *The Bullying Prevention Handbook* by John Hoover and Ronald Oliver. Copyright 1996 by
National Educational Service, 304 West Kirkwood Avenue, Bloomington, IN 47404, 800-733-6786, www.nesonline.com.